Selected poe

Caolán P. Mc

© 2021

Selected poems by Caolán McAleese

I dedicate this book to Nan and Dylan.

Forever in my thoughts.

Selected poems by Caolán McAleese

A Poem for Dylan

A dear son of Lucy and Aidy.

Derek and Helene too.

A doting father to Kayleb and Alfie.

They thought the world of you.

A small man in stature.

But he had a big heart.

He always enjoyed the craic.

It's sad that we must part.

He had his own demons.

A mental war he fought.

But remember all the good days.

And all the joy he brought.

Precious memories to treasure.

Great times we won't forget.

A life well lived and laughed.

Just be glad we met.

But he is at peace now.

No worries, no pain.

Sleep tight Dylan.

Until we meet again.

Cushy

What is there to say?
About the famous Emmett Cushinan.
Your laugh and unique character,
And your cheeky disarming grin.

A cherished son of Henry and Clare.
A dear cousin and a friend.
So many people loved you, Cushy.
Your loss too hard to comprehend.

A family man always,
To Ron and the girls.
A devoted father to Jason.
You meant to them the world.

Your life was far from easy.
But you lived it to the full.
You loved your cars and coffee.
I can't forget your rollies and Redbull.

Selected poems by Caolán McAleese

So many great times with you,

Too many tins and joints.

Precious memories we keep of you,

Up the Lough and at the point.

There aren't many people,

That we meet in life like you.

You were truly one in a million,

A legend through and through!

The Wake

Stern faces,

With welling up eyes.

Long silence broken by a lone ticking clock.

Teaspoons stirring holes in teacups.

Quiet lonely tears and sobbing.

Soft murmurs of short conversation.

Cousins gathering up,

Familiar faces congregating

Round a square box.

Where lays the lady.

Still and cold,

But beautiful.

Finally at peace

The Gentle Giant

The gentle giant sleeps peacefully,

Neath old trees on Cargin Hill.

Gazing over South Antrim vales.

Looking towards Rougery and McLarnon's Mill.

He lies above the old home place.

He's back home now, for good.

His life comes full circle.

His life snuffed out by a lone assassin,

Fourteen shots brough the big man down.

Quick and swift, he didn't suffer.

There is some comfort in that

But he is at rest now,

With Erin's banner at his breast.

Another martyr for old Ireland.

His name added to Roll of Honour.

We shall meet again.

At the Rising of the moon.

Thinking of Thoughts

Thinking, thinking, I am always thinking,

Planning, plotting, over-thinking.

Mind goes a hundred miles a minute,

Never stopping, always thinking.

Thoughts of today and tomorrow,

Pondering the past, with hopes for the morrow.

A never-ceasing mind, ticking like an eternal clock,

Countless ticks, countless tocks.

What stops the mind and its thoughts?

The finality of death.

All thoughts and feelings cease.

Peace at last.

Dark Mind

Waves of negativity cleanse the mind of happiness.

Another period of darkness.

Viewed by tinted eyes,

As if going through life wearing sunglasses.

Making the bright world appear dark in
my mind.

Another bad week, things were going too well.

Followed swiftly by the darkness.

Dragging my spirit back down.

How long will it last this time?

The dark clouds descend again.

Enveloping all that was happy once.

The blackening darkness is here to stay.

When will it get bright again?

Your Own Fight

I tried but I could not,

Be rid of these bad thoughts.

These voices in my head that say,

Begone, and end it all this day.

An unseeable and invisible fight,

That tortures me both day and night.

A war of thoughts swirl in my head,

Screaming and shouting, they wish me dead.

This fight is just for me,

Behind my eyes, for only I to see.

Oh, when will these cruel demons cease,

And give my heart and soul some peace.

But I know I'm not the only one,

Who is fighting hard, but almost done.

Different people, though the same fight,

Who hope and pray for morning's light.

Selected poems by Caolán McAleese

Passing By

Whenever the day is dark,

And the sun falls from the sky.

When I am dead and gone,

Just watch my soul pass by.

Bring me home to dear old Ireland,

Let me wonder through her land.

I wish to dance atop her hilltops,

Whilst holding loved one's hands.

I yearn to see her wild sea again,

And walk from shore to shore.

To gaze along her rugged coast,

From the land that Éire bore.

Oh, just to see my people again,

To laugh, dance and smile.

With my family and friends, a final time,

Oh, to stay for just a while.

Selected poems by Caolán McAleese

But stay here, I cannot,

For I'm only passing by.

I had to see it all once more,

Before my soul could fly.

Selected poems by Caolán McAleese

Think of Me

When I close my eyes on this cruel world,

And bid you all good night.

I'll leave this place once and for all,

And sail far out of sight.

My place, it is not here,

As here, I cannot stay.

I'm on my way to a better place,

I shall not go astray.

But if ye think of me,

Just remember me and smile.

A life laughed and well lived,

But I could only stay a while.

I'm onto the next place,

Wherever that may be.

My time here is up,

Look to the sky and think of me.

Selected poems by Caolán McAleese

I am gone but not too far,

You need only think of me,

And again, I will appear,

For another short time, you'll see.

Selected poems by Caolán McAleese

The Coming Beast

It has no shape or form.

We know not whence it came.

In hell it must been born

Innocent souls it claims.

It levels everything in its path.

Charges forth to fight.

It snuffs out the sun's light.

And all that is bright.

It casts a shadow across the land.

With a thick and darkening black.

A sea of grasping helpless hands.

Oh, when will the sun come back?

It blackens everything.

And takes all joy from life.

A newfound hell it brings.

It bears nothing but strife.

Newfound Hope

But along comes a bit of hope.

Born from years of sorrow.

They came to help their mother cope.

And give her joy for tomorrow.

Alas there comes a sprig of joy,

The birth of a little girl and boy.

Two new lights for this dark life.

To end a mother's tale of strife.

Two new links of an old chain,

To help and ease life's old pain.

Eyes fixed on the coming years.

To smile again and cease the tears.

Two small lights for a dark world,

Through all life's sorrows, tossed and hurled.

Guard these two precious lights,

To carry on their lives so bright.

Path to Peace

Despite all the darkness
There's one thing I know
Is that The sun shall rise
And all the devils will go.

Although the path is dark
And there seems no other way
Continue your journey onwards
To those brighter, better days.

Good shall overcome
And all evils will cease
For a better tomorrow
A mind and soul at peace.

Stay strong and true to yourself
You have all the strength you need
For happier times await you
Where your mind shall be freed.

Selected poems by Caolán McAleese

Keep On Fighting

The battle isn't over
Nor is the was done.
You must keep fighting
Until you have won.

Every day is a battle
Each day of life is a victory
You must push on.
Despite your misery.

Take it one day at a time
Focus on your daily fight
Worry not for tomorrow
Until you feel alright.

Fight the darkness with your thoughts
And with your feelings too.
You can live to see another day.
I have great faith in you.

Inis Taoide

In the wee Lough, there floats an island.

Surrounded by water on three sides.

A forest of headstones and trees.

At its centre, a crumbling church.

Harvey's spire peeks through the treeline.

A modern add on, to St Tida's ancient church.

An eighteenth-century tower crudely sewed on.

Just to please to Earl Bishop upon the hill.

It's an ancient landscape,

Sacred and spiritual for millennia.

St Patrick built here upon Celtic land.

Held dear by the Druids.

One can hear raiding Vikings,

And monks fleeing for their lives.

Or the buzz of American warplanes.

With big-voiced Scullions calling in the cattle.

Selected poems by Caolán McAleese

But its peaceful now,

Loud memories of the past silenced forever.

The birds claim this land now, singing in unison.

With trickling waters caressing rounded stones.

There is solitude here.

To cleanse the mind and soul,

Of the ills of modern-day life.

The Bawn

The Cow Fort stands, four hundred years strong.

Peering over Castle Street.

The Planters fortress,

Whitewashed and crumbling.

Built atop the Celts fort.

A British stamp on an Irish landscape.

The Saxon's are here, here to stay.

Imposing themselves upon the natives.

O'Neill destroyed it in '41, whilst Ulster burned.

Gaelic Ulster was in Rebellion.

These are just memories now,

Etched in her pale stone.

But it's quiet now,

No soldiers or planters.

Just the odd tourist and locals,

Admiring her stern splendour.

Selected poems by Caolán McAleese

Sliabh na gCallan

Black lumps on the horizon

Like shoulders of a giant

Erupt from East to West

From Maghera to Moneymore

Dominating South Derry skies.

At Slieve Gallion

Her highest peak down here

Draws eyes from far and wide.

To the Jewel in South Derry's crown

Bursts out of low laying fields

Going upwards; to the clouds.

River Days

We played at the shallow river,

That snaked through ancient hills.

We ran through fields of green,

In search of any thrills.

We sat upon the wee stone bridge,

And crossed the steppingstones.

We climbed old, crooked trees,

Trying not to break any bones.

We ran for cover from the rain.

And hid neath a blackthorn bush.

To dodge yet another shower,

Cowering under the damp brush.

We skimmed stones across the stream,

Many's an hour passed by.

Slim, mossy rocks we threw,

Under an Irish summer sky.

Selected poems by Caolán McAleese

We galloped through those summer days.

Happy under the beaming sun.

We chased each other and played,

And ran until we were done.

Selected poems by Caolán McAleese

Autumnal Rains

The death of summer gives way to Autumn.

It's only the start now, the impending darkness looms.

The winds are rising as evening light begins to fade.

Memories of summer days seem like history.

The crunch and scent of fallen leaves fill the air.

As near naked trees discard their leaves.

Carpeting the ground with their limbs of gold, amber and rust.

Leaving behind skeletal trees.

Mulch like and decaying.

Conkers and crab apples race to the ground.

Falling to their doom.

Too impatient for human hands.

Nature requires balance with life and death.

There is a chill in the air now, with the smell of rain.

The bright evenings slowly being snuffed out.

Giving way to winters darkness.

Hibernation begins, until nature's rebirth in spring.

Spring has Sprung.

New spring flowers burst forth to meet the brighter days.

Born from darkness, grasping towards spring light.

Winter is gone now, back come the flowers.

Reborn with colours and sweet scent.

Ireland's hedgerows erupt into life.

New growth born out of death.

Green and rejuvenated, ready for another summer.

Come forth the bees and birds,

Ready to suckle at mother nature's new greenery.

Hungry after another bad winter.

Spring has sprung again.

And winter is dead for another year.

To natures delight.

Spring melts into summer.

As Ireland is bathed in sunny rays.

Highlighting her ever-present beauty.

With her many shades of green.

Selected poems by Caolán McAleese

We need the bad days to appreciate the good,

The dull days to savour the bright ones.

The damp days to enjoy the splitting trees.

The winter snow to play in summer sun.

Seasonal balance, nature's eternal way.

Selected poems by Caolán McAleese

Summer Embers

Summer embers ignite the evening sky,

With flames of pink, orange and blue.

A kaleidoscope of colours, blurring and mixing.

To the shepherd's delight.

Sunshine highlights nature's beauty.

Things appear a shade brighter.

More appealing to the eyes.

Winter is gone, be happy.

The sky is naked of clouds.

Big and open, take it all in.

Unmeasurable and boundless,

Stretching far to the universe.

The Winds of Winter

The winter winds rise again.

As her cool winds cut like knives.

Along with her rains.

While Mother nature hibernates,

Yearning for the sunlight.

Patiently waiting for spring.

Bitter cold and wet.

Hibernia indeed,

The land of ever-winter

Fond memories of summer.

Praying for the sun again,

And its companion, the heat.

Counting down to springtime bliss.

Selected poems by Caolán McAleese

Gale

From old Antrim to the States,

Her ancestors left these shores.

In pursuit of a better fate,

The McLeish name they bore.

She's a friend beyond the waves,

An old cousin in a new land.

Her ancestors old and brave,

With deep roots in Ireland.

Bound by blood and name,

Fruit of the same tree.

From a Clan that knows no shame,

We are kin, you and me.

Selected poems by Caolán McAleese

Time

Time waits for no one,

Or yields for anything.

It just passes by,

With more unknowns to bring.

We follow it blindly.

There is no other way.

Onto tomorrow,

For the rest of our days.

It ceases for nothing

And never takes a break.

Onwards we must go,

For our own sake.

On an endless march,

To an unknown place.

Days and weeks pass by,

And leave no trace.

Selected poems by Caolán McAleese

But onward we must go,

Until we finally drop.

To the end of time,

When the clock finally stops.